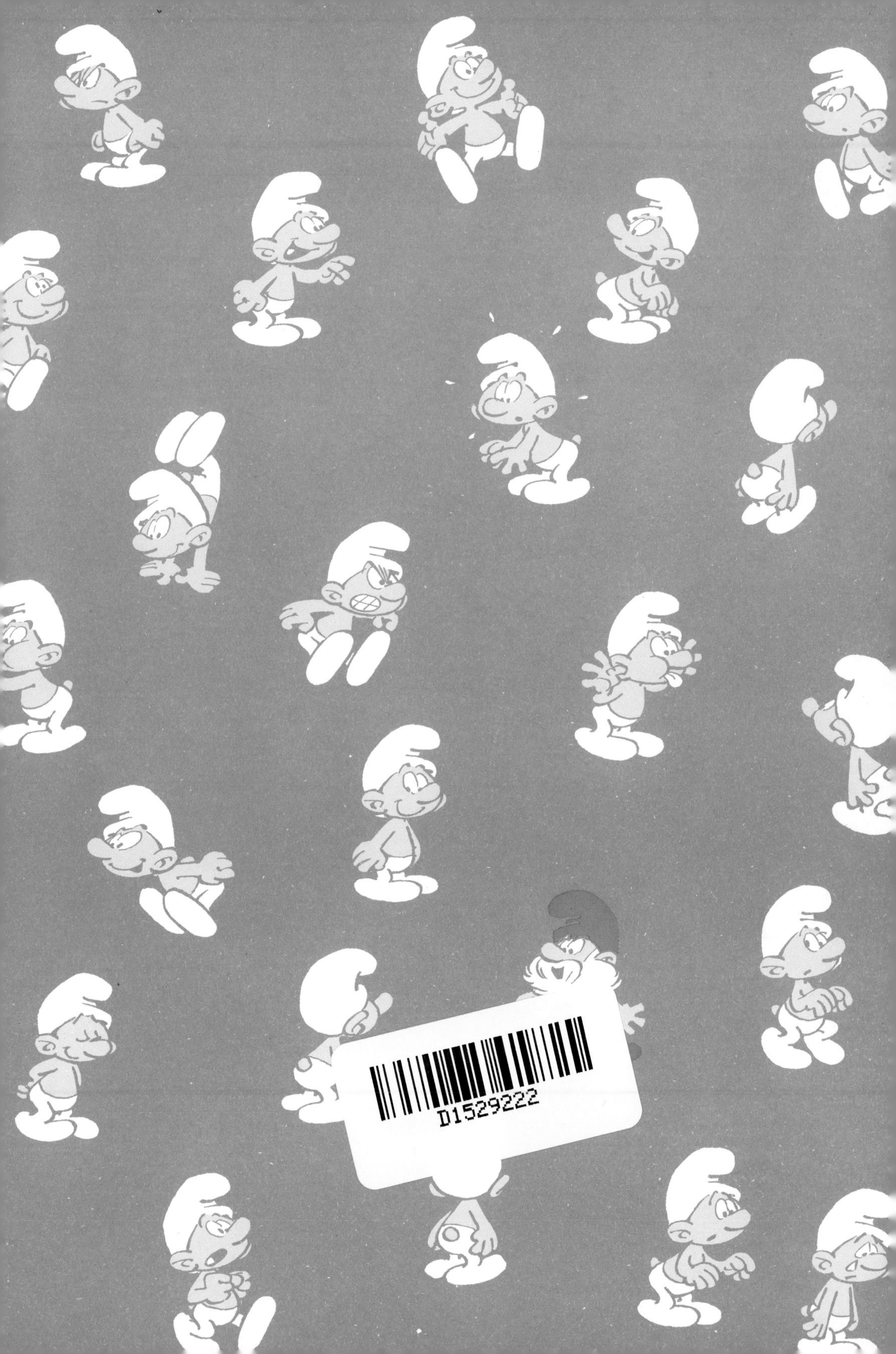

SMURF SALAD

Peyo

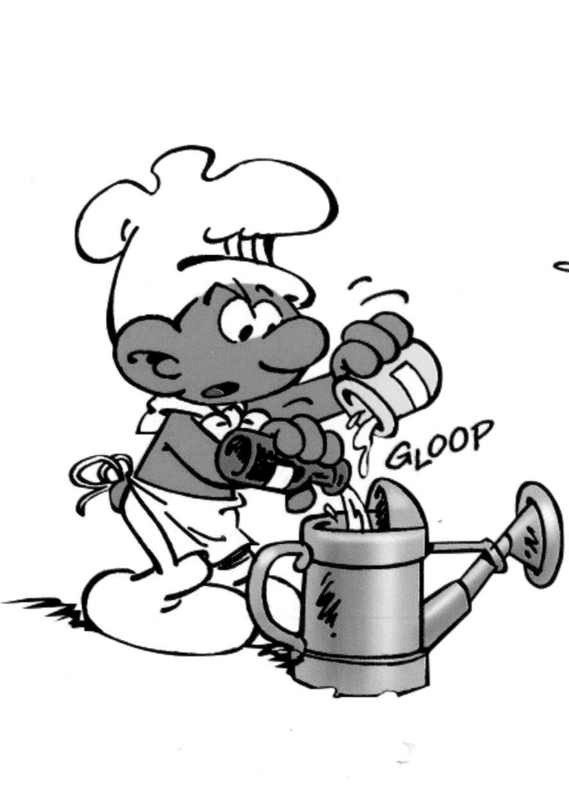
GLOOP

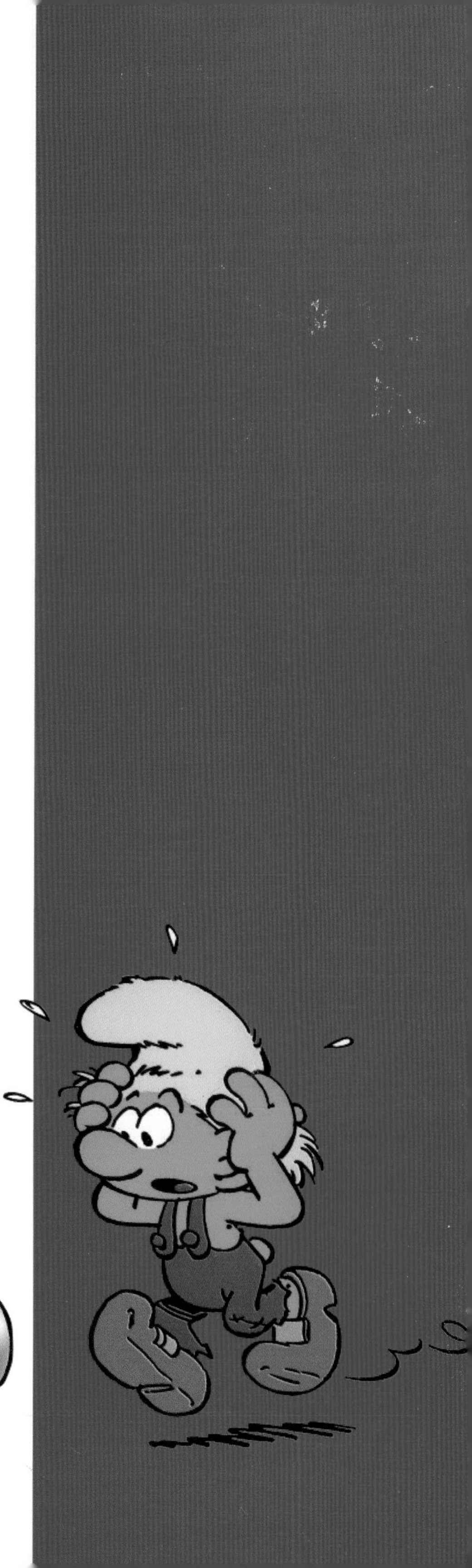

SMURF SALAD

A **SMURFS** GRAPHIC NOVEL BY *Peyo*

WITH THE COLLABORATION OF
LUC PARTHOENS AND THIERRY CULLIFORD – SCRIPT
LUDO BORECKI AND JEROEN DE CONINCK – ART
NINE CULLIFORD – COLOR

PAPERCUTZ™
NEW YORK

SMURFS GRAPHIC NOVELS AVAILABLE FROM **PAPERCUTZ** ™

THE SMURFS graphic novels are available in paperback for $5.99 each and in hardcover for $10.99 each, except for THE SMURFS #21-#26, and THE VILLAGE BEHIND THE WALL, which are $7.99 each in paperback and $12.99 each in hardcover, at booksellers everywhere. THE SMURFS 3 IN 1 are in paperback only for $14.99 each. THE VILLAGE BEHIND THE WALL 2: THE BETRAYAL OF SMURFBLOSSOM is $12.99 each in hardcover only. You can also order online at papercutz.com. Or call 1-800-886-1223, Monday through Friday, 9 – 5 EST. MC, Visa, and AmEx accepted. To order by mail, please add $5.00 for postage and handling for first book ordered, $1.00 for each additional book and make check payable to NBM Publishing. Send to: Papercutz, 160 Broadway, Suite 700, East Wing, New York, NY 10038.

THE SMURFS graphic novels are also available digitally wherever e-books are sold.

PAPERCUTZ.COM

 SMURF ™ **SALAD**

SMURF ™ © Peyo - 2019 - Licensed through Lafig Belgium - www.smurf.com

English translation copyright © 2019 by Papercutz.
All rights reserved.

"Smurf Salad"
BY PEYO
WITH THE COLLABORATION OF
LUC PARTHOENS AND THIERRY CULLIFORD FOR THE SCRIPT
LUDO BORECKI AND JEROEN DE CONINCK FOR ARTWORK
NINE CULLIFORD FOR COLOR.

"The Aerosmurf"
BY PEYO

Joe Johnson, *SMURFLATIONS*
Léa Zimmerman, *SMURFIC DESIGN*
Bryan Senka, *LETTERING SMURF ("SMURF SALAD")*
Janice Chiang, *LETTERING SMURFETTE ("THE AEROSMURF")*
Matt. Murray, *SMURF CONSULTANT*
Izzy Boyce-Blanchard, *SMURF INTERN*
Jeff Whitman, *MANAGING SMURF*
Jim Salicrup, *SMURF-IN-CHIEF*

HARDCOVER EDITION ISBN: 978-1-5458-0335-6
PAPERBACK EDITION ISBN: 978-1-5458-0358-5

PRINTED IN INDIA OCTOBER 2019

Papercutz books may be purchased for business or promotional use. For information on bulk purchases please contact Macmillan Corporate and Premium Sales Department at (800) 221-7945 x5442.

DISTRIBUTED BY MACMILLAN
FIRST PAPERCUTZ PRINTING

COME AND
SMURF IT!

DING
DILING

≥GROAN!≤ Quick! I'm smurfing of hunger!

Stop being dramatic, Greedy Smurf! And don't you think you can smurf my share!

WE'RE-HUN-GRY! WE'RE-HUN-GRY!

That's enough! Smurf right at the table or else I'll tell Papa Smurf!

WE'RE-HUN-GRY! WE'RE-HUN-GRY!

All right, already, it's on the way!

Today we have... vegetable stew!

SNIF SNIF

?

That's it?

Yuck....! It's all dark and smells bad!

© Peyo

5

Here, Greedy Smurf! You can smurf my share!

Really? Thankth!

You can smurf mine too!

Apparently, everyone's not as concerned about the quality of the food!

YUM

SLURP CHOMP

CRUNCH

⇒PFFF!⇐ ...That one would smurf anything!

What's got Chef Smurf smurfing us such disgusting meals?

I don't know, but if he does that again, I'll smurf his face!

And to think now we got to smurf all afternoon with nothing in our bellies!

Me, I don't like smurfing with nothing in my belly!

And consequently, it wasn't a very productive atmosphere at the dam...

The Smurfs aren't very motivated today! There's no use in smurfing them any longer, I'll let them go!

That's all for today! You can smurf!

CLANG DELING

Quick! To Chef Smurf's!

YIPPEE!

Me first! Let me smurf!

© Peyo

2

We're hungry! What's there to smurf?

?

What?! It's the same thing we had for lunch!

WHAT?! AGAIN?

No way! Out of the question!

We don't want any more of that horrible slop!

"Horrible slop"? A little dish I lovingly smurfed over for hours for you?

Next time, you can smurf it yourselves!

Smurf us something else! You're starving us!

?

Leave him to me!

What's all this fuss about?

It's Chef Smurf. Everything he's been making for us lately is DISGUSTING!

He's trying to poison us!

© Peyo

Oh, come now! Aren't you exaggerating a little?

You think so? Well, you have a taste then!

3

⇒Sniff?!⇐
Uh...

Ah!
You see?!

Hmm! You got to admit
your dish has a rather
unasmurfing aroma,
Chef Smurf!

I can't smurf anything
about it, Papa Smurf!
How do you want me
to smurf a good meal
with THIS?!

?

It's true. It's impossible
to smurf anything
whatsoever with such
vegetables!

That's odd of Farmer
Smurf! I'll go ask him for
an explanation!

I don't understand a thing,
Papa Smurf! I smurfed them
all with love! They don't lack
for water or sunshine,
for smurf's sake!

© Peyo

Look! It's so sad
seeing vegetables
in this state!

I'll smurf a few plants to
examine them!

4

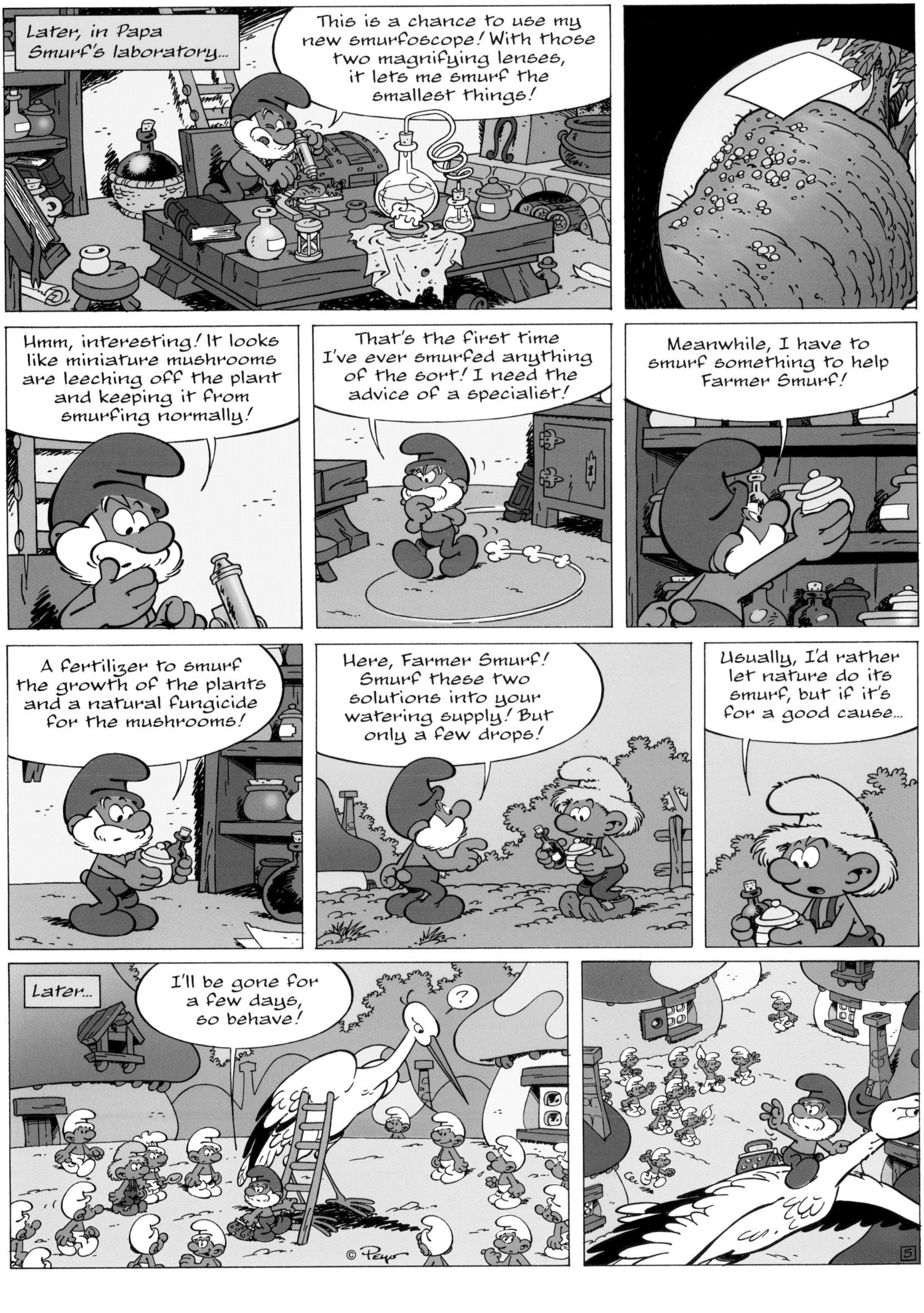
Later, in Papa Smurf's laboratory...
This is a chance to use my new smurfoscope! With those two magnifying lenses, it lets me smurf the smallest things!
Hmm, interesting! It looks like miniature mushrooms are leeching off the plant and keeping it from smurfing normally!
That's the first time I've ever smurfed anything of the sort! I need the advice of a specialist!
Meanwhile, I have to smurf something to help Farmer Smurf!
A fertilizer to smurf the growth of the plants and a natural fungicide for the mushrooms!
Here, Farmer Smurf! Smurf these two solutions into your watering supply! But only a few drops!
Usually, I'd rather let nature do its smurf, but if it's for a good cause...
Later...
I'll be gone for a few days, so behave!
?
© Peyo
5

All right then, Papa Smurf did say: "Only a few drops!"

Let's hope that will smurf some effect!

Later...
→Psst!← Farmer Smurf! Do you have a few minutes?

Uh... When will the vegetables you smurfed with Papa Smurf's solutions be ready?

Oh, that... you know how it's smurfs with vegetables! We got to wait a few days!

A FEW DAYS?!
Why, that won't do at all!

You absolutely must smurf them as fast as possible! Look at what I got!

?

Change menus or you'd better smurf out!

Are you sure you smurfed enough solution on your vegetables?

?

I'm certain we must smurf more!

Hey! Papa Smurf said--

POP

ARE YOU CRAZY?!

Well, Papa Smurf isn't here and he's not the one risking his smurf! Here goes... maximum dose!

And that one too!

Come on, Farmer Smurf, if it were dangerous, do you really figure Papa Smurf would've smurfed you all those solutions?

And above all, if you do nothing, they're going to come bust my smurf!

Oh, too bad then! I'll just resmurf home and sadly await my fate! ⇒BWWAAAH!⇐

Uh... Wait, Chef Smurf! Maybe you're right! I'll go smurf a bigger dose on the vegetables!

I knew I could smurf on you!

I'll even help you water your garden!

The next morning...

⇒YAWN!⇐ All right, get to smurf!

POW

Golly gee smurf! What ✿⑥☀! Smurf smurfed this joke on me?

11

Well, now! You see there wasn't anything to smurf about!

You can't convince me that all this isn't very smurf!

And at noon...

Today on the menu, a mega vegetable stew! Dig in!

YUM-YUM!

8

© Peyo

CHOMP GULP GULP YUM YUM SLURP CRUMPF

Aaaaah, I haven't smurfed like that in a long time! Now for a good nap!

Excellent idea! →Burp!← Sorry!

Oh, you, restorative slumber
Who, after such a fine meal,
Smurfs us an hour
Our wearied limbs to heal.

That was pretty good, Poet Smurf!

Hey?! What do you have on your nose?

I don't know. Looks like a pimple!

HA!HA! HA!HA! HA!

Poet Smurf's breaking out in pimples! He's smurfing like a teenager to us!

That evening...

I ate too much! And that always smurfs me restless! A little stroll will smurf me good!

?!

CRAC

13

Uh... is someone there?

→Gulp!← This alley is spooky!

Bah! My imagination is surely smurfing tricks on me!

CRAC

I'm sure of it this time! Someone's there. I heard smurfing!

I... I saw you! Is that you, Jokey Smurf?! Go on, come out of the shadows!

AAAAAH!

A week later...

Ah, what a joy it is to smurf home and see the Smurfs again!

The village is intact! For once, it looks like the Smurfs behaved themselves during my absence!

Well, now! I was expecting a different sort of welcome!

10

© Peyo

14

HEY! IS ANYONE HERE?!

What's with all this mess? Where have they all gone?

Of course, my good little Smurfs must be smurfing on the dam!

Or on the bridge over the Smurf River! That must be it...

Alas, Papa Smurf's hopes are dashed...

So, the Smurfs aren't at the dam or the bridge, or even at the lake smurfing around being lazy. What could have happened?

Gargamel! That must be it! He must have smurfed a way to capture all the Smurfs!

But at Gargamel's...

I swear I'll get revenge on those cursed blue gnomes!

The problem is how do I trap those vermin without knowing the location of their village?

© Peyo

11

15

Well, no Smurfs here! Strange!

I'll continue my search tomorrow! It's getting late, and I'm hungry! I haven't smurfed anything since this morning!

Hey! Apparently Farmer Smurf has solved his vegetable problem!

Mmm... Not bad!

?

— CRAC

That noise! It's my little Smurfs coming back!

Nobody?! But I'm sure I heard smurfing! Anyone there?

Is that you, Papa Smurf?

Is it really you?

© Peyo

Who else would it be?

12

YIPPEE! Papa Smurf is back!

We're saved!

?!

What a welcome! You're very kind! I'm happy to see you too!

CHOMP! CHOMP!

But tell me what smurfed here? Where have the others gone?

They've been smurf vegetabl... First then ne... that's when the Poet...

Yes! And Hefty Smurf said we had to smurf him in the storeroom and then...

Uh, one at a time!

No, it was Brainy murf who said that! And...

Let's smurf inside, you can tell me this more calmly!

A few moments later...

So here goes, after we smurfed uh... a little... hmm!.... of your solution on Farmer Smurf's crops, the harvest was smurfly abundant...

13

17

"And the Smurfs ate their fill once again...

Aaah... That's what you call a real meal! Thanks, Chef Smurf!

Uh... Heh heh! it's nothing, my friends, nothing!

Greedy Smurf, how can you still eat after such a meal? Nobody smurfs sarsaparilla anymore anyways!

I love it! It's like a little dessert!

"But that evening...

HELP! HELP! Chef Smurf!

BAM BAM BAM

?

There's a monster out there! It's enormous and completely green!

Enormous and completely green?!

What's smurfing? What's all the noise?

Sounds like someone smurfed someone!

It's Scaredy Smurf. He says he saw a monster!

?

It's true!

Ha ha ha! A monster! That's a good one!

It was in the little alley!

YAWN!... Go ahead, show us! Then we can smurf back to bed soon!

14

?!

Aaah... There! You see?

© Peyo

18

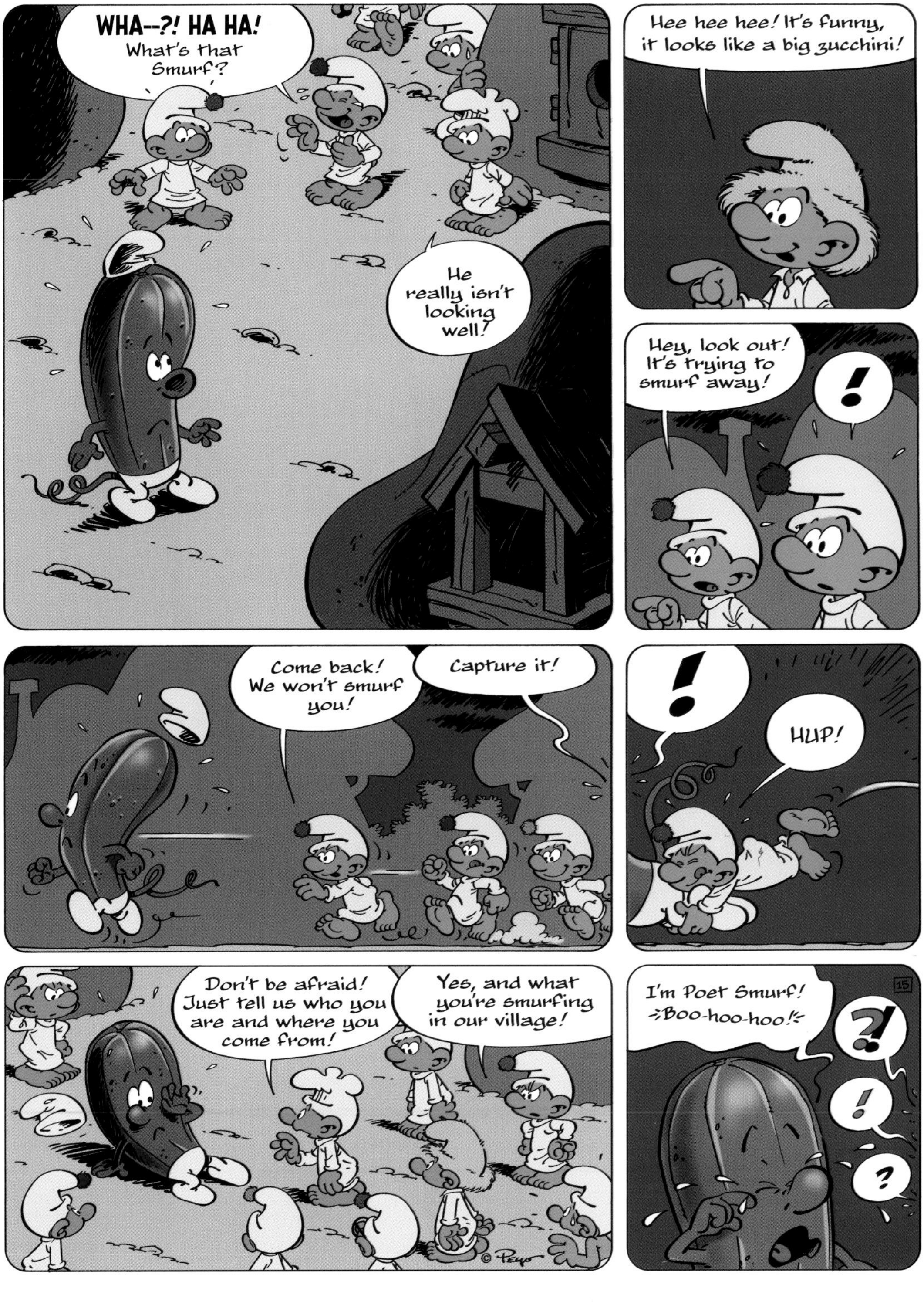
WHA--?! HA HA! What's that Smurf?
He really isn't looking well!
Hee hee hee! It's funny, it looks like a big zucchini!
Hey, look out! It's trying to smurf away!
!
Come back! We won't smurf you!
Capture it!
!
HUP!
Don't be afraid! Just tell us who you are and where you come from!
Yes, and what you're smurfing in our village!
© Peyo
15
I'm Poet Smurf! Boo-hoo-hoo!
?!
!
?

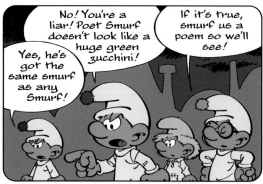

No! You're a liar! Poet Smurf doesn't look like a huge green zucchini!

Yes, he's got the same smurf as any Smurf!

If it's true, smurf us a poem so we'll see!

Oh, thou who... ⊰Sniff⊱ ... wert handsome, Now thou art ill-favored... ⊰Sniff⊱

Hey, it's true that, if you smurf your eyes, you'd think you were listening to a bad poem by Poet Smurf!

Well, what happened to you then?

I have no smurf! When I went to bed, the green pimple on my nose was itching me a lot...

I woke up soon after! My bed had gotten too small! So I went to smurf at myself in the mirror and saw this horrible face! I thought it was a nightmare and I smurfed out of my home! And that's when I ran into Scaredy Smurf!

But it wasn't a nightmare, and I've really become a monster!

Well, my smurfness! What a story!

Do you all think I'll stay like this forever? Farmer Smurf, you know about vegetables... What do you think?

I sure do know my vegetables, but I've never seen a zucchini smurf all by itself!

Papa Smurf will know better than me!

© Peyo

16

Hmm... If I may be allowed, I think I'm just as capable of smurfing this problem! And like Papa Smurf always says: "Never smurf off until tomorrow what you can--"

POW

We'll wait for Papa Smurf's return then!

The next day, the whole village was smurfed around Zucchini Smurf... uh... Poet Smurf!

"Some even used the opportunity to make fun of his smurf...

Poor Poet Smurf!

That's what smurfs when you want to be the top banana!

Jokey Smurf, that's not very smurf of you!

HA! HA! HA! HA! HA!

It's true! Here... to apologize for myself! Don't worry, it's not a firesmurfer!

SPROTCH

© Peyo

I wanted to smurf some butter on the spinach! But I forgot you were a zucchini!

HA! HA! HA! HA!

17

HA! HA!
HA!
HA!

?

What is it, Greedy Smurf? Do you want to smurf fun of me too?

No, I was just wondering what a zucchini in butter would taste like!

Yum! Yum!

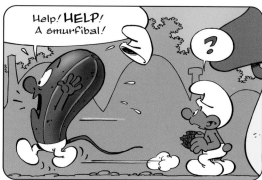

Help! HELP! A smurfibal!

?

"But the mockery soon ended, because the next day...

Help! I'm a tomato! I'm a tomato!

You got to smurf something! Help me!

We said we'd wait for Papa Smurf to get back. Anyhow, it's not so bad, Poet Smurf! Yesterday, you smurfed into a zucchini, today into a tomato, maybe tomorrow--

18

?!

YOU DON'T GET IT, I'M NOT POET SMURF! I'M JOKEY SMURF!

© Peyo

22

EEEEEEEEEK!

That's Smurfette!

She's in danger, for smurf's sake!

HOLD ON, SMURFETTE! WE'RE COMING!

There's a pickle in my laundry!

Who are you? Don't be afraid. Come out of there!

Yes, show your vegetable smurf!

÷Bwwaaaah!÷ I'm Vanity Smurf! I was so embarrassed of being smurfed as a pickle, I hid myself!

What's smurfing on here?

Jokey Smurf and Vanity Smurf have smurfed into vegetables!

There's three of them now!

Look at this horrible green tint and all these bumps on my smurf!

Bah! Smurf yourself in a little vinegar, and nobody'll notice! Whahaha!

This is getting worrisome! We got to smurf something!

Let's smurf a meeting!

© Peyo

"So, a meeting presided over by Hefty Smurf was smurfed...

Quiet, please! Quiet!

I SAID QUIET!

BLA BLA SMURF BLA

BLA BLA BLA

BLA BLA

BLA BLA

BLA BLA

BLA

BLA

BLA

BLA BLA

Thank you! We've gathered here to smurf this problem preoccupying us, which you all know about!

Uh... I don't really see what you're smurfing about!

Dopey Smurf, you leave, or else we'll never get anything done!

Hey, can you smurf a little less loudly? I'm trying to sleep!

You too, Lazy Smurf. OUT!

Really! We're here to smurf serious things!

So then, can anyone explain what's happened to our three friends?

20

© Peyo

24

ME! I'd like to smurf something even if you never listen to what I smurf and, what's more, if Papa Smurf were here, it wouldn't smurf like that!

Could someone shut him up and smurf him outside?

But I think there's another question we should smurf!

That question is: "Why did they smurf one after the other and not all three at the same time?"

? ? ? ?

That's true! He's right for once!

Yesterday, Poet Smurf's the one who turned into a zucchini...

Yes, and today, Jokey Smurf and Vanity Smurf!

Maybe they're contagious!

? ? !

CONTAGIOUS?!

?!

© Peyo

[21]

Well... What then, my friends?

Don't come any closer, Jokey Smurf!

If you take another step, I'll smurf my smurf in your smurf!

?!

You might contaminate us! And we'd be smurfed into vegetables too!

Yes, we have to quarantine them!

WHAT?!

Quarantine us?

You don't have the right to smurf that! Papa Smurf is the village leader and he isn't here!

You're right, Jokey Smurf! So we'll smurf a vote by raising hands!

Don't worry! With all the friends we have, we have nothing to fear!

All those who agree they should be quarantined, smurf your hand!

I thought we had friends?

Uh...

© Peyo

26

And you all let that happen!

But Papa Smurf... Let's just say... We didn't want to be smurfed into vegetables!

You too, Smurfette?

Uh... it was a democratic vote!

And where did you smurf them?

Uh... Well, in the storeroom!

Just you wait till Papa Smurf comes back...

Right! Get in and shut up!

Someone will smurf you food through the hole that was smurfed in the bottom of the door!

Here, Dopey Smurf, you'll smurf here and guard them! They mustn't get out!

Me?! But I don't want to smurf into a vegetable!

Just don't get near them, and nothing will happen to you!

Being in the dark is bad for my complexion!

When I smurf, I smurf with you, Liberty!

This isn't funny!

Was it really necessary to lock them up, Hefty Smurf?

It was to protect all of us, Smurfette! You wouldn't want to be smurfed into a pickle!

© Peyo

23

"But the next morning, when I was smurfing their food...

I smurfed a bit of soup for you!

Hey, where has your guard Dopey Smurf smurfed?

Heh heh! Surprise!

?

Uh... Chef Smurf?

WHAAAH! A potato-smurf?

Something funny happened to me last night!

Help! He's been smurfed into a potato!

Hey, wait!

ZIP

He didn't give me time to smurf him what happened to me!

You'll have plenty of time to talk once you're with us!

With you? What do you mean?

Think, idiot! You've become a vegetable like us! What do you think they'll smurf to you? Make fries?

You... You think that --?!

No way, I don't want to be locked up with you!

24

© Peyo

28

There he is! We got to smurf him or he'll contaminate the whole village!

Quick, smurf somewhere to hide!

Greedy Smurf, you haven't seen Dopey Smurf?

Yum. Nope!

Where could he have smurfed?

On the other hand, I did see a potato smurf by!

!

!

That's the spitting image of Dopey Smurf!

Do you think they'll capture him?

÷Brrr!÷ This story smurfs chills down my spine!

Look, there they are! Hefty Smurf smurfed him!

÷Bwwaaaah!÷ I don't want to be smurfed in the storeroom!

25

29

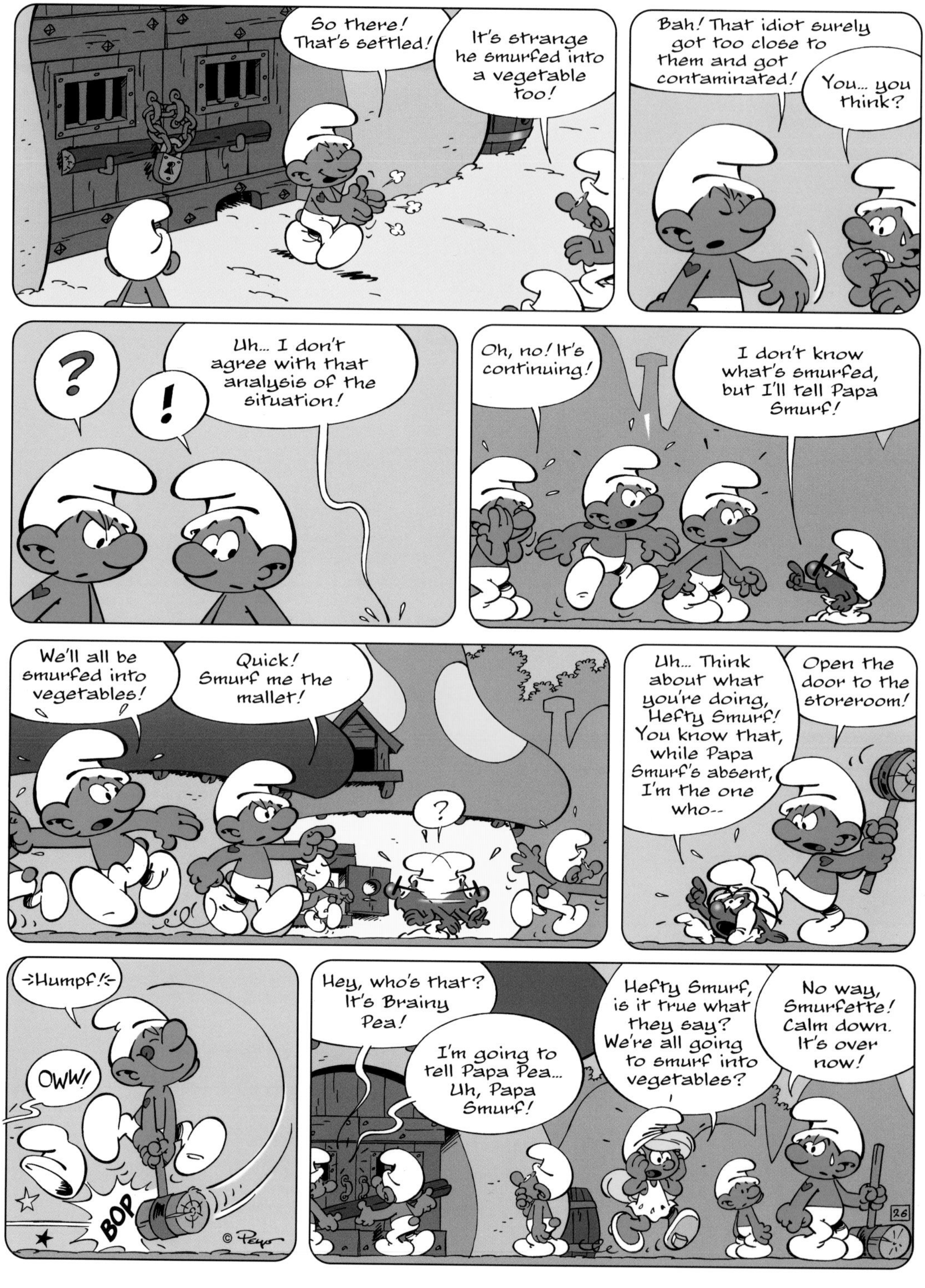
So there! That's settled!
It's strange he smurfed into a vegetable too!
Bah! That idiot surely got too close to them and got contaminated!
You... you think?
?
!
Uh... I don't agree with that analysis of the situation!
Oh, no! It's continuing!
I don't know what's smurfed, but I'll tell Papa Smurf!
We'll all be smurfed into vegetables!
Quick! Smurf me the mallet!
?
Uh... Think about what you're doing, Hefty Smurf! You know that, while Papa Smurf's absent, I'm the one who--
Open the door to the storeroom!
Humpf!
OWW!
BOP
© Peyo
Hey, who's that? It's Brainy Pea!
I'm going to tell Papa Pea... Uh, Papa Smurf!
Hefty Smurf, is it true what they say? We're all going to smurf into vegetables?
No way, Smurfette! Calm down. It's over now!
26

"Unfortunately, it was only beginning...

I'm a cabbage! I'm a cabbage!

"Those who smurfed into vegetables were immediately hunted down...

"...and locked away with the others!

"Some smurfed masks to try to protect themselves from the illness...

"...But it was no use!

"The storeroom continued to fill!

Make room, please!

You pack of smurfs, you wait till we get out of here!

Hey! Take your hand away from there, if you don't want the back of mine upside your smurf!

"Until the day when it was Hefty Smurf's turn to be smurfed...

Oh, no!

"So we were the last four left!

© Peyo

27

What? You want to smurf me in the storeroom with the others?

Well... Uh...

Hefty Smurf, surely you wouldn't want me to turn into a carrot?

You're right, Smurfette!

I'll go smurf myself into the storeroom on my own!

Ha! Ha! Ha! We knew it'd be your turn one day!

Did you see your eggplant mug? You're a monster like us now!

You'll see what it's like being locked up!

Oh! Well, darn it!

CRAC

YEEAAAAH!

COME ON! EVERYONE OUT! YOU'RE FREE!

!?

© Peyo

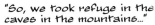

Smurf them! Let them become monsters like us!

AAAAAH! I don't want to become a monster!

"So, we took refuge in the caves in the mountains..."

Since then, we've been smurfing to the village from time to time at night, waiting for your return!

And where are the other Smurfs now?

Uh... They smurfed into the forest, but we don't know where!

Hmmm... Okay! We'll see about that later! Let's smurf instead to the bottom of these transformations!

Let's start by going to smurf at your garden, Farmer Smurf!

Uh... now, Papa Smurf? ...In the dark of night?

The sun is up! Let's go!

Soon after...

It's just as I thought!

© Peyo

Farmer Smurf, I told you: "Only a few drops!"

I... I was pressured, Papa Smurf!

Pressured? By whom?

"..."

Chef Smurf! Can you please stay with us?!

Heh heh heh! Uh... ⇒Gulp!⇐

So, it seems you influenced Farmer Smurf so he'd smurf more solution on his vegetables?

Ohh! He's exaggerating, Papa Smurf! It was just one or two extra drops!

One or two! Yeah, my smurf!

Just go ahead and say it's my fault!

It sure is!

That's enough! Now's not the time!

We'll resmurf this later! The important thing is to understand what happened to the others and find out how to cure them!

What's the connection with the garden?

I think eating these mutant vegetables is what smurfed the Smurfs!

© Peyo

30

What makes you believe that, Papa Smurf?

You four, for example! You haven't been smurfed! Have you eaten those vegetables? You, Farmer Smurf?

Oh! I ain't much for all those un-natural smurfs! So I don't touch 'em!

And you, Chef Smurf?

You know... Hmm... When you smurf in the kitchen all day long, you don't really feel like eating your own cooking!

Hee hee!

Smurfette?

Let's just say I'm in the middle of a diet...

Fine! Fine! That confirms my suspicions!

I'll smurf a piece of this squash and analyze it in my laboratory!

Later...

I hope Papa Smurf will find an answer quickly!

Laboratory

NO SMURFING

All this because of a certain Smurf who--

31

© Peyo

35

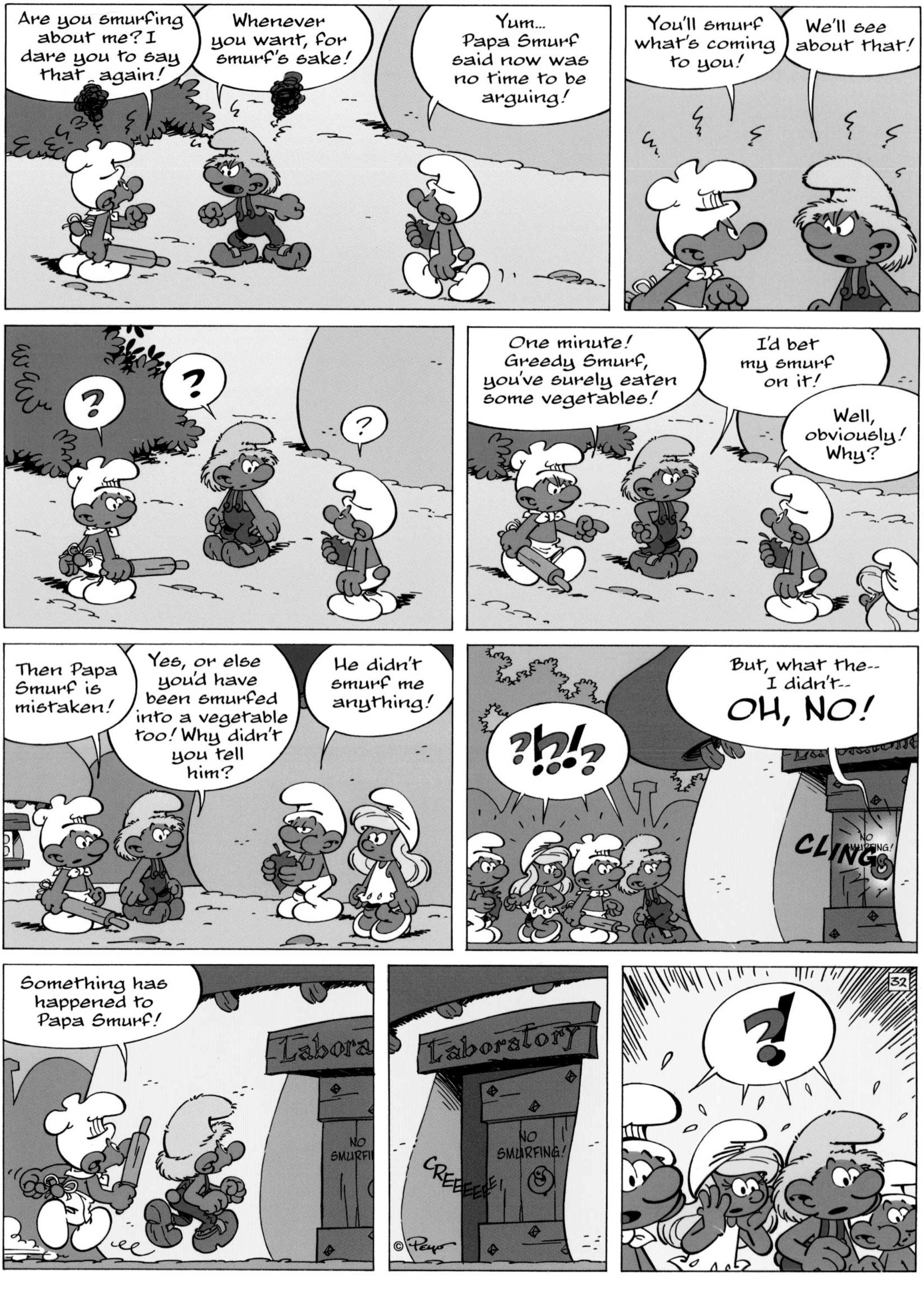
Are you smurfing about me? I dare you to say that again!
Whenever you want, for smurf's sake!
Yum... Papa Smurf said now was no time to be arguing!
You'll smurf what's coming to you!
We'll see about that!
?
?
?
One minute! Greedy Smurf, you've surely eaten some vegetables!
I'd bet my smurf on it!
Well, obviously! Why?
Then Papa Smurf is mistaken!
Yes, or else you'd have been smurfed into a vegetable too! Why didn't you tell him?
He didn't smurf me anything!
?h!?
But, what the-- I didn't--
OH, NO!
CLING
Something has happened to Papa Smurf!
Laborat
NO SMURFIN
Laboratory
NO SMURFING!
CREEEEEEE!
© Peyo
32
?!

I don't understand!

AAAAAH! Papa Smurf changed too! Run!

No, wait! There's surely an explanation!

How is this possible? It doesn't smurf with my theory!

But... But yes, of course!

Last night, after coming back from Gargamel's, I ate a little soup!

Now I just have to go smurf the others in the forest!

HEY! WHERE ARE YOU?

-PFFF!- ... What will we smurf now that Papa Smurf has smurfed into a vegetable too?

Hey! Did you hear that?

It's Papa Smurf! He's gone in search of the others!

© Peyo 33

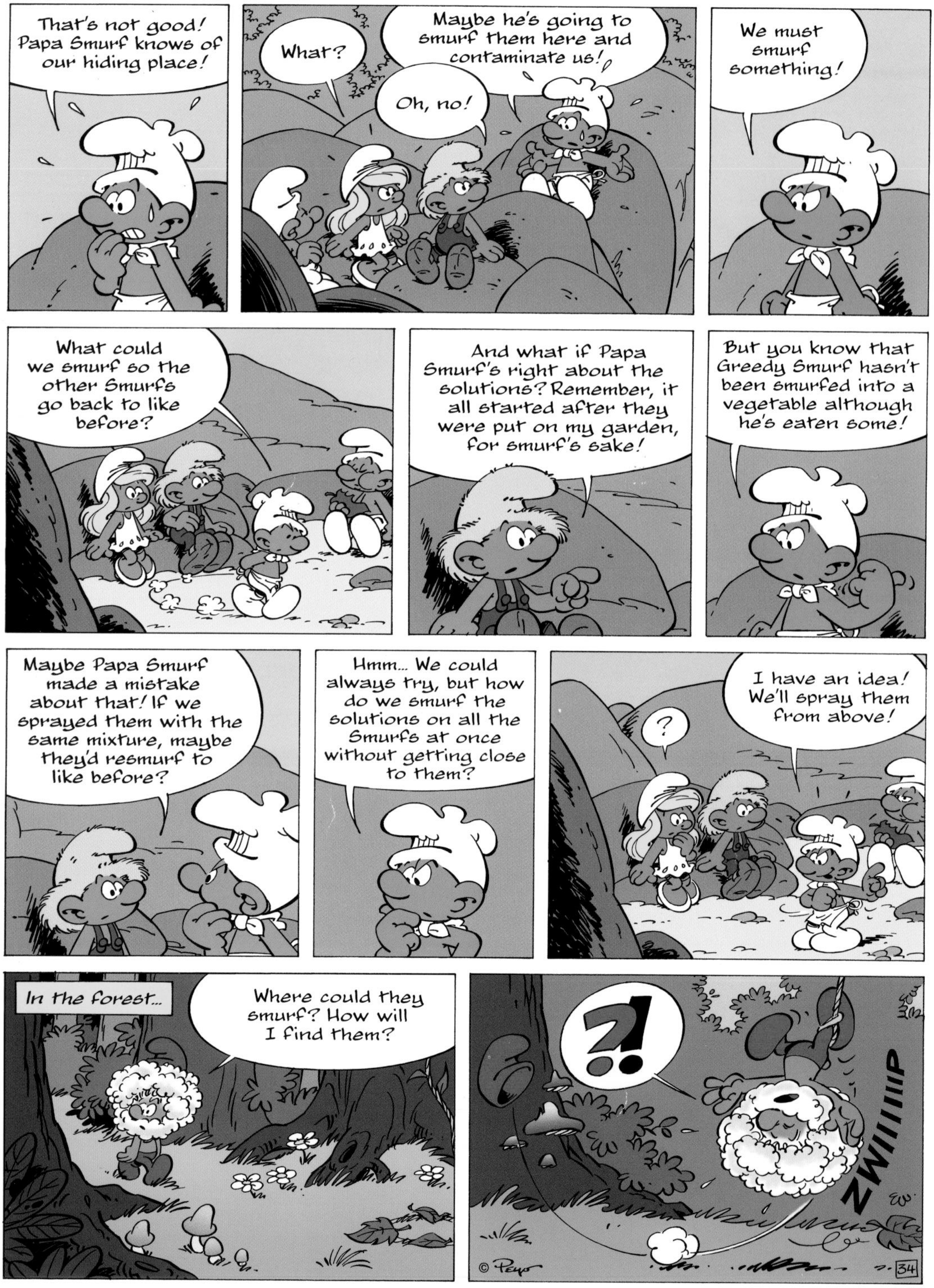
That's not good! Papa Smurf knows of our hiding place!
What?
Maybe he's going to smurf them here and contaminate us!
Oh, no!
We must smurf something!
What could we smurf so the other Smurfs go back to like before?
And what if Papa Smurf's right about the solutions? Remember, it all started after they were put on my garden, for smurf's sake!
But you know that Greedy Smurf hasn't been smurfed into a vegetable although he's eaten some!
Maybe Papa Smurf made a mistake about that! If we sprayed them with the same mixture, maybe they'd resmurf to like before?
Hmm... We could always try, but how do we smurf the solutions on all the Smurfs at once without getting close to them?
?
I have an idea! We'll spray them from above!
In the forest...
Where could they smurf? How will I find them?
?!
ZWIIIIIIP
© Peyo
34

What the smurf--?! What smurfed?

WE GOT ONE!

That trap was a good idea, Handy Smurf!

Don't forget I'm the leader!

Let's smurf him! Let him become a vegetable too!

Huh? It's already done!

That's funny, he reminds me of someone!

If Papa Smurf were here, he'd smurf you a lesson! Since he isn't--

But I am Papa Smurf, you pack of two-legged veggie-smurfs! Smurf me down from here!

Papa Smurf is back!

YIPPEE!

Thanks, my friends! But let me speak! I must smurf you something important!

♪ Papa Smurf is back! Papa Smurf is back! ♪

BOP

?

Go on, Papa Smurf! Go on!

Mmm...

I've discovered it's the food that smurfed us into vegetables! Let's go back to the village. I'll find a way to cure us!

© Peyo

35

39

Yippee! We're returning to the village!

If it's the food, it's Farmer Smurf and Chef Smurf's fault!

When I catch them, I'll show them!

Meanwhile, at the village...

Nobody's here! We can go in!

Are you sure of what you're smurfing, Chef Smurf?

If you have a better idea, don't hold back!

I just hope that... →Gnnn!←... Help me smurf the door!

CREEEE

Heh heh! I knew Aerosmurf's* plane was still in the hangar!

And there's my big spray can that I smurf once a year for weeds!

Perfect! Go smurf the solutions Papa Smurf gave you for your garden and find a larger quantity in his laboratory!

36

*see THE SMURFS #16 "The Aerosmurf" or page 50.

Smurfette, if you wouldn't mind smurfing watch... In case the veggie-smurfs come back!

Of course!

Greedy Smurf, help me smurf the sprayer onto the plane. Afterwards, we'll push it out!

Here are the two flasks Papa Smurf smurfed to me. Quick, to the lab!

"Fungicide" and "natural fertilizer," that's them!

Here goes! Both of 'em in this bottle!

GLUG GLUG

I hope this'll do the job!

Hey! What the-- THE OTHERS! THE VEGGIE-SMURFS!

Look over there! Farmer Smurf!

It's his fault we're like this! Smurf him!

No, wait!

CHARGE!

37

© Peyo

41

When I say "contact," you just have to grab the propeller and smurf it really hard! Okay?

LOOK OUT! THE VEGGIE-SMURFS ARE HERE! WE'VE GOT TO SMURF!

Quiiick! They're coming!

Everyone, into the plane!

Greedy Smurf, you see to the propeller!

GO AHEAD! "CONTACT"!

VRRRR

Look! They're trying to get away!

Uh... It may be time for us to go!

VRRRRRRRR

Here goes!

?

38

Chef Smurf, I think we've forgotten Greedy Smurf!

?

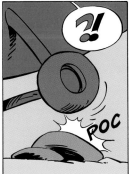

?!

POC

LOOK OUT! SMURFETTE!

Hey, the bottle!

IIIEEEE!

It's okay! Got 'er!

You have Smurfette?

Uh... No! The bottle!

We've got to smurf back for Smurfette!

Too late! I'm lifting off!

VVVVRRRRR

ASSASSINS!

?

IIIIEEEEE! I'll be smurfed into a vegetable!

Have no fear, Smurfette! That won't happen to you. It's not contagious!

But what about you, Papa Smurf?

I'm like this because I ate some of the soup last night!

But Greedy Smurf smurfed some soup, too! Why is he still normal?

?

Greedy Smurf? For smurf's sake, I hadn't paid him any mind! Come here! Don't be scared!

It is strange! But my analyses were clear, it's because of the food! There must be a reason!

What are you smurfing there? Sarsaparilla?

Yep! It's like a dessert to me and it's good for digestion!

Did anyone smurf any sarsaparilla just before or after becoming a veggie-smurf?

Uh... no!

Nope!

No, and you?

No!

No!

Hmm, hmm! Interesting! What if...?

Hmm... I'll go smurf some tests! Nobody bother me!

Uh... Papa Smurf, I must smurf you something about Chef Smurf and Farmer Smurf!

What's wrong, Smurfette?

They have a plan to cure you! They want to spray on all of you a large quantity of the same stuff you gave to Farmer Smurf for his garden!

!

But that could be smurfly dangerous for all of us!

40

© Peyo

44

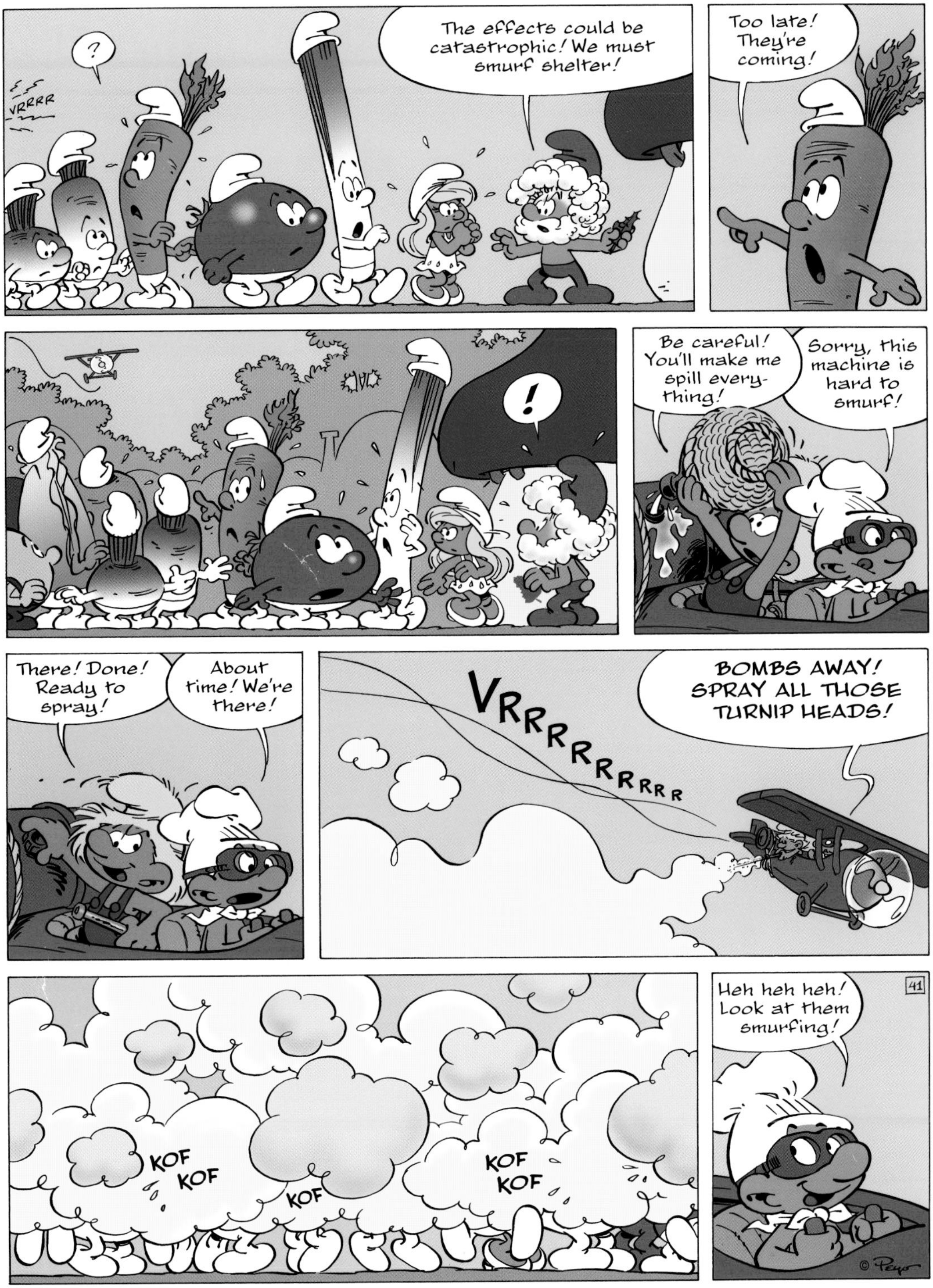
VRRRR
?
The effects could be catastrophic! We must smurf shelter!
Too late! They're coming!
!
Be careful! You'll make me spill every-thing!
Sorry, this machine is hard to smurf!
There! Done! Ready to spray!
About time! We're there!
VRRRRRRRRR
BOMBS AWAY! SPRAY ALL THOSE TURNIP HEADS!
KOF KOF
KOF
KOF KOF
41
Heh heh heh! Look at them smurfing!
© Peyo

Our only chance is that sarsaparilla is the antidote! Otherwise, we'll be smurfed into vegetables permanently!

KOF KOF

YUM YUM

EUREKA! One bite is enough!

IIIEEE!

Look! They're acting weird!

⇒Buh!⇐

Greedy Smurf! Do you still have sarsaparilla leaves?

⇒Buh!⇐

?

KOF KOF

I have a few left in my pocket!

Smurf me half of it! Along with Smurfette, give the rest to any veggie-smurfs you run into!

Here, Jokey Smurf! Smurf this!

⇒Buh...⇐ I'm siiiiick... ⇒Yum!⇐ ⇒Yum!⇐

Yippee! I'm myself again! Who wants a gift?

You see anything in that pea soup?

Hey! Look out!

THE CHIMNEY?!

© Peyo

CRAC

42

46

Pull up!

Impossible! Look out, we're going to smurf in your garden!

SPROTCH

You're the last, Brainy Smurf! Here, smurf this!

→Groan!← ...Like Papa Smurf always says, the last shall be first!

Papa Smurf! Chef Smurf and Farmer Smurf crashed into a pumpkin!

There they are!

→Kof! Kof←! Yuck, there's pumpkin everywhere! I swallowed a lot of it!

→Gulp!← Me, too! →Kof! Kof!←

They'll get what's coming to them!

This is all their fault!

Let's get out of here!

I feel... →Kof← ...weird!

→KOF! KOF!←

WHAAA! HA! HA!

Hee Hee Hee!

What? What's wrong?

Why are you laughing?

AAAH!

Hey! You've gone back to normal!

It's thanks to me! My plan worked! The solutions we sprayed smurfed you back into Smurfs!

Not at all, Chef Smurf! You nearly smurfed great danger to all your friends!

Oh? Uh... We thought we were doing good!

Luckily, you know the antidote! You can smurf us back to our normal selves!

Yes, that's true!

Certainly, but I think staying in the form of vegetables for a while will smurf you a good lesson!

!

Later...

Your vegetables look good, Farmer Smurf! Too good to be true!

No, no! I assure you! I've smurfed only natural things on them!

It's been a week now, Papa Smurf! Couldn't we go back to being Smurfs again?

I'll think about it!

44

© Peyo

END

48

Welcome to the totally transformative twenty-sixth SMURFS graphic novel by Peyo, from Papercutz, those fast-food connoisseurs dedicated to publishing great graphic novels for all ages. I'm Jim Salad-crop, er, I mean, Jim Salicrup, the Chef Salad-loving Smurf-in-Chief, er, I mean, Chief. I'm here to share a few thoughts on Fruit and Veggie-Smurfs, share some exciting Smurf news, and tell you about another comics sensation we're sure you'll enjoy…

But first, let's talk about "Smurf Salad," shall we? While there are always folks around complaining how bad everything in the world has become, there are also many great things happening every day. Just in the field of nutrition, we know far more now than we ever have before. Back when I was a kid, we acted as if we could eat anything in moderation with little or no serious consequences. While my favorite breakfast cereal was *Kellogg's Rice Krispies*, with added banana slices, I did occasionally indulge in *Sugar Pops, Sugar Smacks,* and *Fruit Loops,* to name just a few. Obviously, with many of these cereals back then the major attraction was sugar, and as we realize today, too much (and exactly how much is too much?) sugar is just not healthy for you.

There was even an official Smurfs cereal during the run of the animated Smurfs cartoon show back in the 80s. *Smurf Berry Crunch* debuted on supermarket shelves in 1983, followed years later by *Smurf Magic Berries*. The advertising jingle was set to the tune of Tchaikovsky's *The Nutcracker Suite*…

> "*Smurf Berry Crunch* is fun to eat.
> A Smurfy fruity breakfast treat
> Made by Smurfs so happily.
> It tastes like crunchy Smurf Berries.
> It's berry-shaped and crispy too.
> In berry red and Smurfy blue."

See! How can you possibly resist that? The Smurfs themselves eat a much healthier diet, consisting mostly of various fruits and vegetables, although they do enjoy a Smurf baba (a rich cake soaked in rum and sugar syrup) every now and then. But that was then, and this is now. Although in "Smurf Salad" we never found out why the vegetables in Farmer Smurf's garden had gotten so bad in the first place, I think we learned that there can be awful side effects when tampering with Mother Nature's way of doing things.

And speaking of Mother Nature, it was recently announced that the Smurfs will be helping save the planet in two big ways. First, the Smurfs join the European Union's fight against ocean waste by taking part in the Global Beach Cleanup campaign in 140 countries around the world. Véronique Culliford, daughter of Peyo, joined João Aquiar Machado, director-general for fisheries and maritime affairs for the European Commission to sign the agreement. Sec-

ond, the Smurfs have joined the firefighters and national fire safety associations for the #Together4FireSafety campaign in Europe in order to improve fire safety in buildings for people. I guess that even includes Gargamel!

Papercutz is incredibly proud to be publishing THE SMURFS, not just because the characters are doing their part to save the planet, but because THE SMURFS are simply wonderful comics, the creation of Pierre Culliford, better known as Peyo. Recently, Papercutz through its Charmz imprint, has had the honor of publishing the work of yet another internationally acclaimed cartoonist, Mauricio de Sousa from Brazil. He created MONICA, a brash little girl with a plush blue bunny and her gang of friends. Charmz will be publishing the teenage version of this character in MONICA ADVENTURES. For more on this exciting comics event, see the bonus feature starting on page 58.

But back to THE SMURFS…as another extra bonus, we're representing the entire "Aerosmurf" story starting on the very next page. Why? Well, if you enjoyed "Smurf Salad," you already know the answer, and if you haven't, we don't want to offer any spoilers. And wasn't it spoiled veggies that started everything in this book? So, no spoilers, but be sure to look out for the next SMURFS graphic novel, and the all-new Smurfs animated series, both coming soon.

Smurf you later,

STAY IN TOUCH!

EMAIL: salicrup@papercutz.com
WEB: papercutz.com
TWITTER: @papercutzgn
INSTAGRAM: @papercutzgn
FACEBOOK: PAPERCUTZGRAPHICNOVELS
FANMAIL: Papercutz, 160 Broadway, Suite 700, East Wing, New York, NY 10038

THE AEROSMURF

by Peyo

Do you remember the Flying Smurf? (¹) Do you think he's forsaken his idea of rising up into the sky? Well, no! He's still thinking about it...

Ah! Icarus! What a lovely dream!

When suddenly, that morning...

Why, yes! How come I didn't smurf of that sooner?

I'll need Handy Smurf's help.

Handy Smurf, you have to smurf me a hand-to-smurf machine that'll smurf me into the smurf...

?

Hold on... I'll make you a blueprint...

Mmm, yeah... in theory, it ought to smurf, but I'd need some light wood, canvas, leather, rubber, screws, springs...

I'll look for all that!

And late into the night...

When will that racket be over?

BING
TCHOOF
BING
TZEEEEEEEE
DZEEEEEE
BING
BANG

(¹) From THE SMURFS #1, of course!

The next morning...

HEY!

?

Everybody come! Check out the marvelous invention I smurfed last night!

? ?

What's that smurf?

It's an aerosmurf! A machine that's going to let me fly, thanks to its wings and a big rubber band that'll smurf the propeller!

?

Well, my smurf...

Do you really think that'll smurf?

Heavier-than-air!

He's going to bust his smurf!

Obviously!

Okay, I'll wind up my machine!

GRR?

GRRRR

Watch out! Smurf back! I'm smurfing for take-off!

Me, I don't like take-offs!

FRRRRRRR

2

It works! **I'M FLYING! I'M FLYING!**

Bravo! It smurfs!

He got something heavier-than-air to fly!

I said it would smurf!

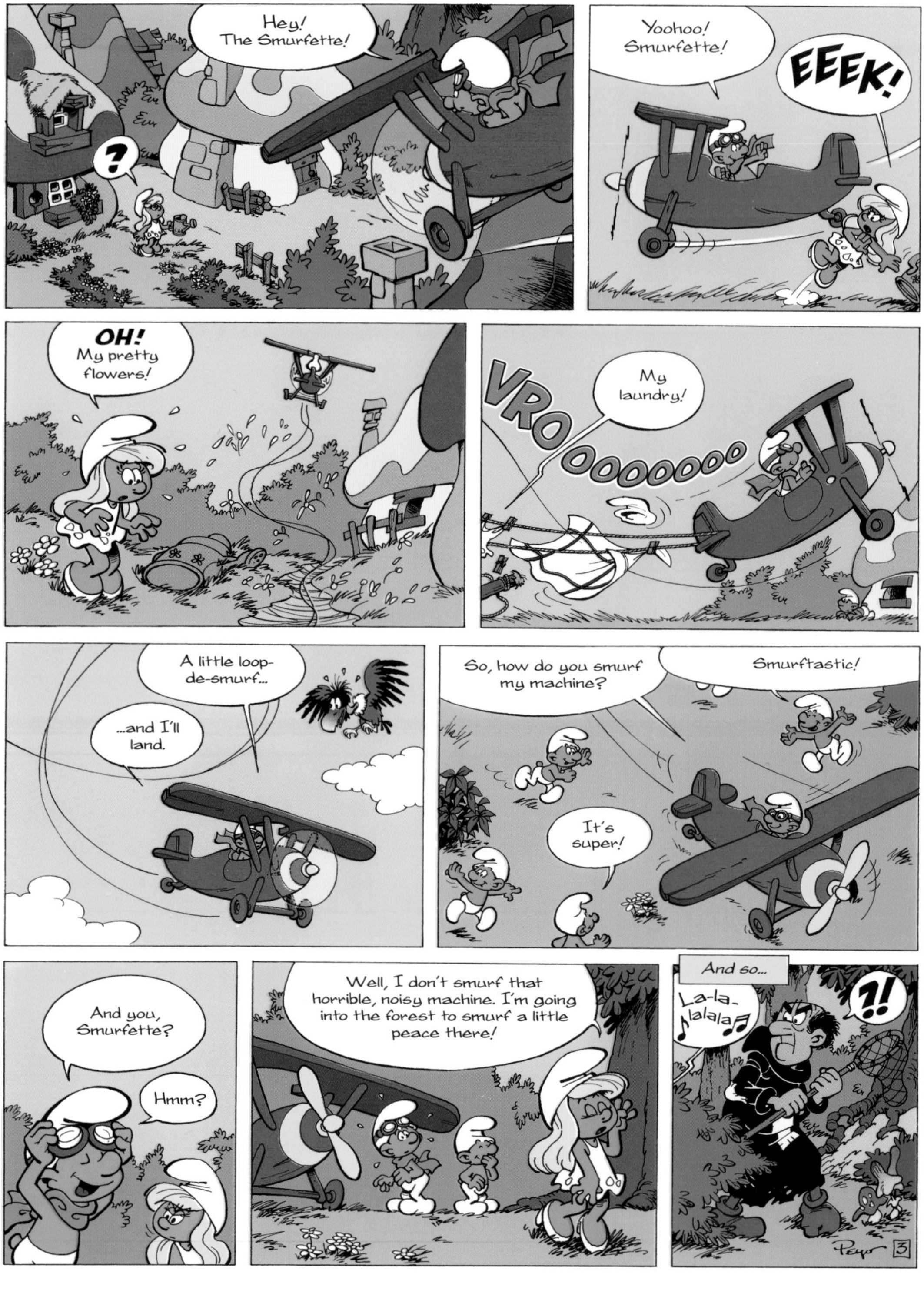
Hey! The Smurfette!
?
Yoohoo! Smurfette!
EEEK!
OH! My pretty flowers!
VROOOOOOOOO
My laundry!
A little loop-de-smurf...
...and I'll land.
So, how do you smurf my machine?
Smurftastic!
It's super!
And you, Smurfette?
Hmm?
Well, I don't smurf that horrible, noisy machine. I'm going into the forest to smurf a little peace there!
And so...
La-la-lalala
?!
Peyo
3

Why look who's here! It's that charming, little Smurfette! Heh heh heh!

♪La-la-la la la♪

GARGAMEL!

Heh heh! I've got you!

Let me go, you big brute! You boor! Or else I-- I--

Yeah! Yeah!

SCRATCH SCRATCH

Hello, pretty little crow!

?

Go quick and carry this to the Smurf Village!

÷Cawwww...!÷ Does he think that I'm some kind of carrier pigeon?

And now, let's go home and wait for them to get my message!

Later...

That's strange. Smurfette's not back.

Look, a crow with a message in its beak!

It's from Gargamel! He's smurfed Smurfette and will only resmurf her in exchange for her weight in gold.

But we don't have any gold! She's doomed!

No! I'll save her! Quick! My aerosmurf!

FRRRRRRr

Peyo

4.

53

There's his hovel! But where can he be?

There! There he is! About time!

?

What's that dirty, little fly?

Why it's a Smurf!

VRRRR

Get! Scram! Shoo!

Oops!

Smurf tight, Smurfette!

EEEEE!

My hero!

My smurfette!

Give her back, you dirty, little upstart!

What's happening?

The motor's winding down! We're falling!

FLIPPLEFFFFF

Take the controls! I'll try to resmurf it while flying!

EEEEEEEE! But I've never smurfed before!

HA! HA! He's losing altitude! I've got him!

SPUT SPUT SPUT

Peyo

5

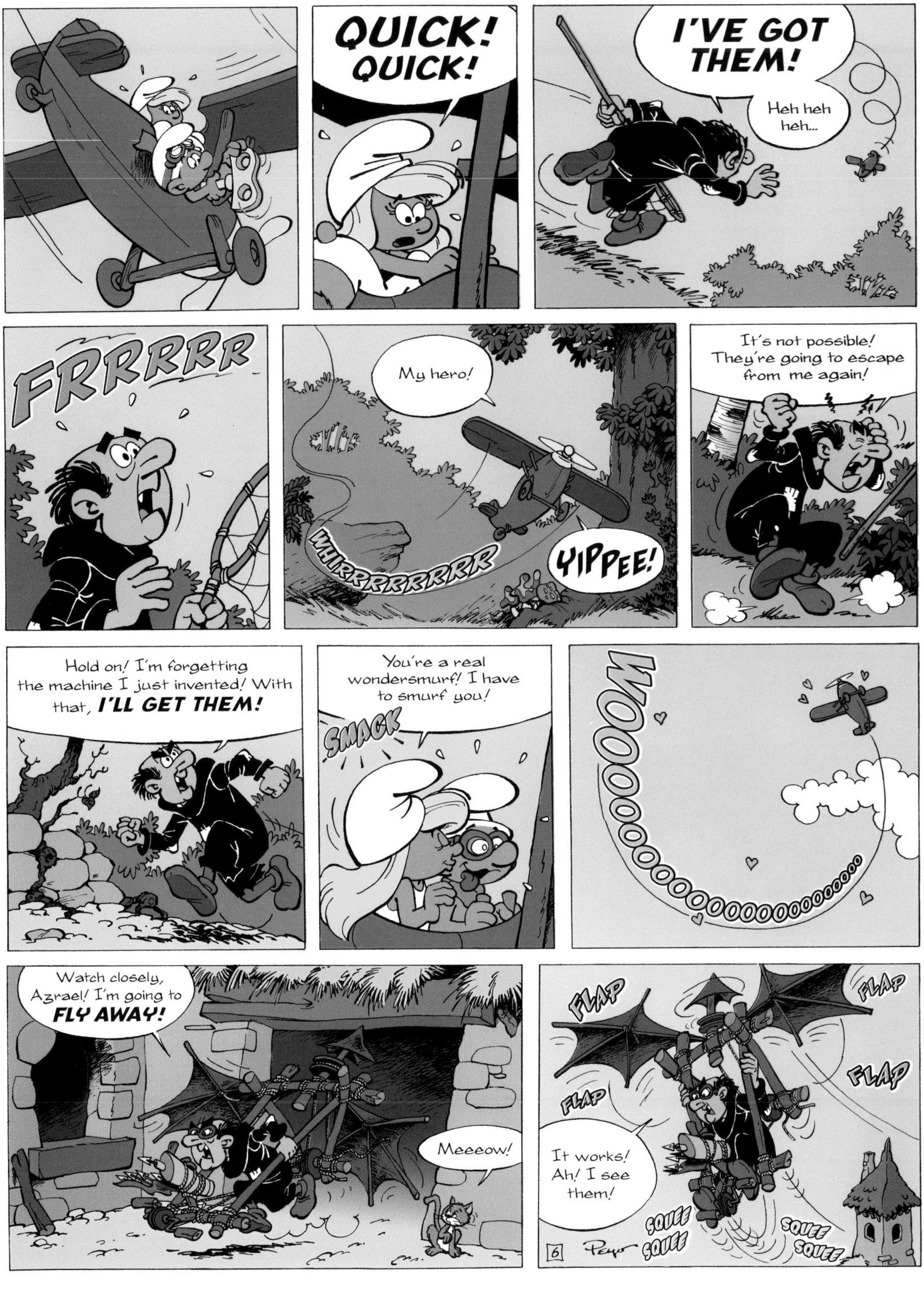
QUICK! QUICK!
I'VE GOT THEM!
Heh heh heh...
FRRRRR
My hero!
WHIRRRRRRRRR
YIPPEE!
It's not possible! They're going to escape from me again!
Hold on! I'm forgetting the machine I just invented! With that, I'LL GET THEM!
You're a real wondersmurf! I have to smurf you!
SMACK
WOOOOOOOOOOOOOOOOOOOOOOOOOOOOOOM
Watch closely, Azrael! I'm going to FLY AWAY!
Meeeow!
FLAP
FLAP
FLAP
FLAP
It works! Ah! I see them!
SQUEE SQUEE
SQUEE SQUEE
6
Peyo

EEEEEEEEEE!
Behind us! It's Gargamel!

FRRRRRR

FLAP FLAP FLAP

HEH HEH HEH!

SQUEE SQUEE

I've got you now! I just have to aim straight!

TAC TIKKATIKKA

ZWING ZWING

ZWING ZWING

ZWING

Why-- why he's smurfing at us!

THOK

THUK

We can't stay in front of him! Hang on!

What will you do?

CHUK

FLAP FLAP FLAP

?

A few aerobatics...

SQUEE SQUEE

We got him! Smurf me the packages!

?!!

FLAP FLAP

SQUEE

Yoohoo! GARGAMEL!

?

Here's a gift for you! Hope you like it!

Peyo 7

A gift? That's nice! I wonder what it is...?

BOOM

Hey! Here's another one! And another! And another!

BOOM
BOOM
BOOM
BOOM

Aaaah! I can't see!

HELP!

CRASSH

I'll get you! I'll get you!

Flying Smurf, you've smurfed my life. Once we land, I'll smurf you something...

Oh, boy!

Smurf me now...? Smurf me now...?

Now you're going to resmurf all of my laundry! And then you'll resmurf my flowers! You'll resmurf my damaged chimney! And next...

END

Monica
Adventures

Meet Monica.

She is fierce, confident, and super strong. She won't put up with anyone teasing her or her friends. She's always been like that…

Monica's first appearance in Jimmy Five's newspaper strip on March 3rd, 1963. Even if you don't speak Portuguese, you can see the start of this comic rivalry.

Charmz, is proud to publish Monica's adolescent adventures in the United States and Canada for the first time. Monica and her gang have been friends for years, since childhood. Now, join Monica and her gang of friends as they take on all the ups and downs of high school life including dating, social media, crushes, gossip, or just finding the cash to enjoy a night at the movies.

There's a lot to love about Monica. We asked celebrated comics writer Gail Simone for a blurb announcing Monica's arrival on the North American comics scene and here's what she wrote: "The international phenomenon comes to America, with all the charm, fun, and cuteness intact. Monica's here, gang!"

As Gail said, Monica is an international phenomenon. For example, Monica and J-Five have hobnobbed with *Astro Boy* and other classic manga characters such as *Kimba the White Lion* and *Princess Knight*. Mauricio de Sousa, Monica's creator, was a personal friend of their creator, the late master of manga, Osamu Tezuka. He even has a cameo in MONICA ADVENTURES #1!

Osamu's cameo.

Not to be outdone, Monica then helped save the universe by teaming up with none other than the *Justice League*! That's right! Monica has met *Wonder Woman, Superman, Batman,* and all the rest. These adventures are only available in Brazil so far, but who knows what the future may bring?

MONICA is actually one of the first ladies of comics. Created by legendary Brazilian cartoonist Mauricio de Sousa in 1963, her comic adventures as a young, super-strong girl in her neighborhood have taken most of the world by storm since her debut. Monica has been translated to 14 languages and has appeared in 40 countries and counting!

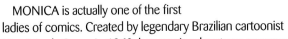

CLASS IS OUT EARLY, I GUESS. SEE THAT?

SEE HOW ESSENTIAL THESE *SITES* ARE?

ESSENTIAL, YEAH...

... FOR THOSE THAT LIKE MEDDLING IN OTHER PEOPLE'S LIVES.

FINE, *HUN!* ACT LIKE A SAINT ALL YOU WANT, OKAY?

I SAW YOU LIKE THAT POST FROM YOUR PHONE!

U-UM... IT'S JUST... WELL...

LET'S GET ONE THING STRAIGHT, OKAY?

EVEN MO' GIGGLED A BIT.

SHE'S TOTALLY ALL ABOUT THE DRAMA... IT'S TYPICAL BAGGAGE OF BEING A PRINCIPAL CHARACTER

WELL, I...

WAIT A MINUTE! WHAT DO YOU MEAN?!

I'M JUST SAYING THAT THERE IS NOWHERE TO HIDE, PUMPKIN!

YA'LL CAN PRETEND AS MUCH AS YOU'D LIKE...

...BUT THE WORLD REVOLVES AROUND SOME JUICY GOSSIP!

RIGHT! I HAVE TO ADMIT, IT REALLY WAS FUNNY...

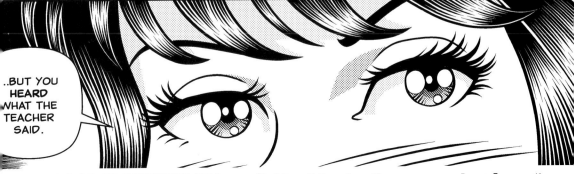

..BUT YOU HEARD WHAT THE TEACHER SAID.

MONICA ADVENTURES #3 is available at booksellers everywhere!

Now, thanks to resident Monica fan, managing editor Jeff Whitman, Charmz is bringing Monica to the USA and Canada. "In Brazil, Monica is everywhere you look, from diapers to headlining Comic Cons that rival the big ones here. She is the bestselling brand in Brazil and it is virtually impossible to avoid her influence there," said Jeff. "Her comics are pure enjoyment, with a robust cast of colorful characters you can identify with, zany plots spoofing or parodying all genres, and with a gentle reminder of how it is to be a kid. She is timeless. I knew her adventures as a teenager, presented in a manga-like style, would be perfect for North American audiences.

There's humor, drama, and a whole lot of heart. It is an impressive repertoire that we are just beginning to scratch the surface of. Creator Mauricio de Sousa, his daughter (the real-life inspiration behind Monica!), and the whole studio in Brazil has welcomed Charmz and

MONICA creator, Mauricio de Sousa, with Monica fan and Charmz editor, Jeff Whitman.

me with open arms. Bringing these wonderful comics to the United States and Canada was the next logical step for Monica and her friends!"

Monica and her gang aren't kids anymore in MONICA ADVENTURES. But things haven't changed much as Monica got older. Jimmy-Five now goes by J-Five but still gets tongue-tied around Monica. Instead of teasing her, he pines for her, and hopes to be as successful as her one day. Maggy tries to eat healthier these days, and Smudge has accepted the necessity of a shower, but old habits die hard!

Nancy and Sluggo, Lois and Clark, Jane and Tarzan, Monica and Jimmy Five…some classic comics couples.

Monica first appeared as a young girl in the comics, always running her block as the girl-in-charge. Super-strong, with a short temper and a rather short stature, she was the perfect target for the conniving, but lovable, Jimmy Five (the five stands for the amount of hairs on his head), and his best friend Smudge, who is certifiably afraid of water, to come up with all sorts of maniacal and "infallible" plans to usurp Monica as the leader of their group of friends. Plans, which Monica usually can thwart with her eyes closed and some help from her blue plush rabbit (that doubles as a dangerous projectile), Samson. Add in Monica's best friend, the always-famished Maggy, and some other unforgettable and relatable neighborhood kids and the recipe (calm down, Maggy, not that kind of recipe!) for fun is endless.

J-Five and Smudge are bigger comicbook nerds than anyone we know!

Already picked up the first two volumes of MONICA ADVENTURES and want more Monica now without having to take an intensive Portuguese class? Head over to YouTube and check out the "Monica Toy Official" channel to see hundreds of videos of Monica and friends. The best part? The videos have no words! Monica's comedic timing needs no explanation! While you're there, tell them your friends at Charmz sent you!

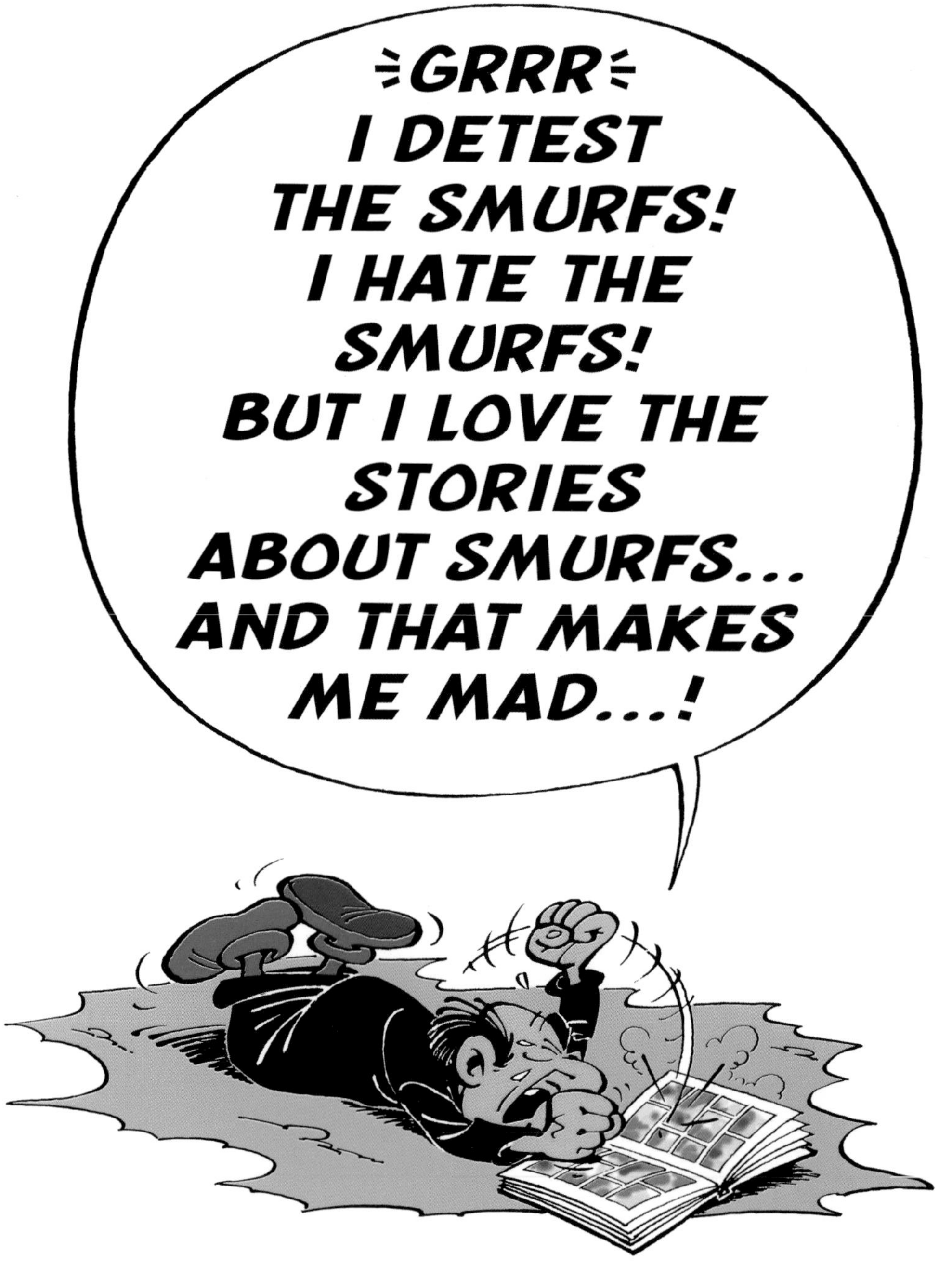
GRRR
I DETEST THE SMURFS! I HATE THE SMURFS! BUT I LOVE THE STORIES ABOUT SMURFS... AND THAT MAKES ME MAD...!

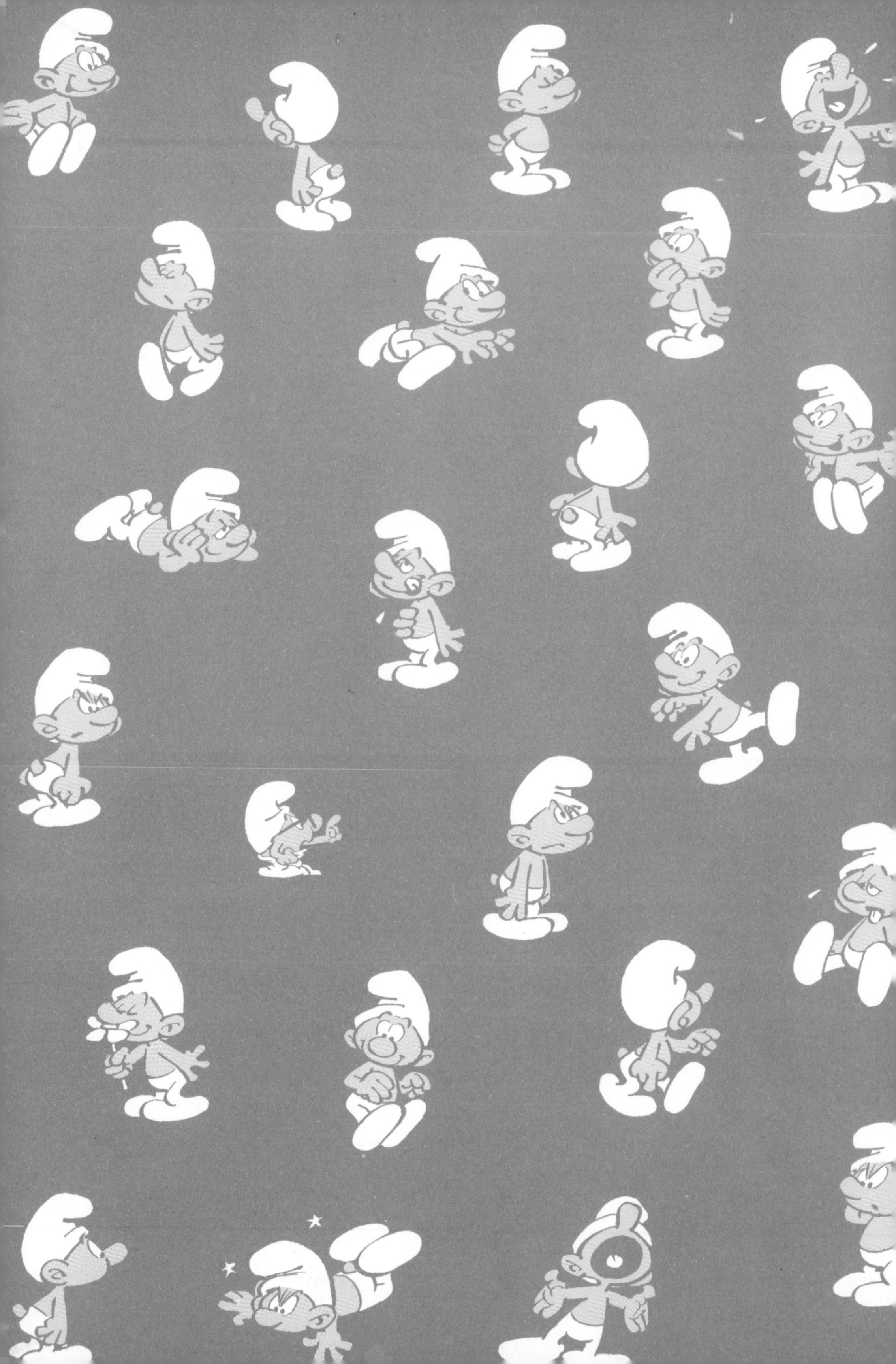